S0-ADZ-713

The Boxcar Children Mysteries

THE TATTLETALE
MYSTERY

created by
GERTRUDE CHANDLER WARNER

Illustrated by Hodges Soileau

SCHOLASTIC INC.
New York Toronto London Auckland Sydney
New Delhi Mexico City Hong Kong Buenos Aires

ISBN 0-439-43394-0

12 11 10 9 8 7 6 5 4 3 2 1   2 3 4 5 6 7/0

Printed in the U.S.A.   40
First Scholastic printing, January 2003

Contents

CHAPTER 1

Who Threw That?

"I sure hope it flies!" cried six-year-old Benny as he jumped to his feet. "Do you think it will?"

"There's only one way to find out," said Henry, who was fourteen. "Toss it in the air and see what happens."

It was a warm August afternoon and the four Alden children — Henry, Jessie, Violet, and Benny — were in a little park on the edge of the town of Greenfield. They were making paper airplanes while their dog, Watch, dozed in the sun nearby.

"I guess you're right, Henry," said Benny. "There's only one way to find out." And he tossed his paper airplane into the air. "Look!" Benny began hopping up and down excitedly. "It's flying!"

"Way to go, Benny!" Ten-year-old Violet clapped her hands and cheered.

Jessie, who was twelve, gave her little brother a thumbs-up. "Great job, Benny!"

Watch, who was awake from his nap, went racing across the park. A moment later he came running back with Benny's airplane in his mouth. Wagging his tail, the dog dropped the airplane at Benny's feet.

"Thanks, Watch!" As Benny bent to pick it up, a frown crossed his round face. "Uh-oh."

"What is it, Benny?" Jessie asked.

"Watch chewed it up a bit," Benny told her. "I don't think it'll fly anymore."

"Never mind, Benny." Violet had folded a square sheet of purple paper into the shape of an airplane. Then she drew a rainbow pattern on the wings with her colored pencils. "You can have this one when I'm done," she offered. Violet was artistic and liked making beautiful things.

Sitting down again, Benny shook his head. "That's okay, Violet." He shoved the chewed-up airplane into his back pocket. "I can make another one in no time." And he reached for another sheet of paper.

"Just remember," said Jessie, who often acted like a mother to her younger brother and sister, "the important thing is to make sure the corners and the ends of the paper fit together when you make the folds."

Violet looked up and waved to Mrs. Spencer. Mrs. Spencer was a neighbor and a good friend of the Aldens. She lived across the street from the park, and today the children had helped her bring groceries home from the supermarket. Now she waved to them from her front porch.

"Why don't you come and get some lemonade before you go," she called.

"Oh, thank you, Mrs. Spencer," said Jessie, walking up the steps with her brothers and sister. "We could use something cold right now."

Mrs. Spencer poured lemonade into tall glasses. Then she sighed and smiled. "Watching you in the park cheers me up a bit. I remember my school days with my best friend, Milly Manchester. I used to pass her messages — on paper airplanes!"

"Really?" Benny stared wide-eyed. "Did you ever get caught?"

"Yes, I did," Mrs. Spencer replied as she made herself comfortable on a porch chair. "And the teacher made us stay after school. We had to write *I will not throw paper airplanes in school* a hundred times on the blackboard."

"Wow!" Benny's big eyes grew even rounder. "I bet that took a long time."

Henry, Jessie, and Violet laughed. They couldn't imagine Mrs. Spencer throwing paper airplanes. She was such a sweet lady, and it was hard to think of her getting into trouble at school.

"Have we ever told you about *our* old days, Mrs. Spencer?" Jessie asked. "When we lived in the boxcar?"

"Why, your grandfather told me. It

sounds like quite an adventure!" said Mrs. Spencer.

After their parents died, the four Alden children had run away. For a while, their home was an old abandoned boxcar in the woods. But then their grandfather, James Alden, found them, and he brought his grandchildren to live with him in his big white house in Connecticut. Even the boxcar was given a special place in the backyard. The children often used it as a clubhouse.

"Did our grandfather tell you about Watch?" Benny wanted to know. "About how we found him when we were living in the boxcar?"

Jessie smiled. "Mrs. Spencer knows, Benny," she said. "And she knows how lucky we are to have Grandfather and Mrs. McGregor now, too." Mrs. McGregor was the Aldens' housekeeper and a wonderful cook.

"Speaking of Mrs. McGregor," said Benny, "it's almost time for — "

"Lunch," Violet finished for him.

This made everyone laugh. The youngest Alden was *always* thinking about food.

"Making paper airplanes gives me an appetite," Benny said with a grin.

"*Everything* gives you an appetite, Benny!" Henry teased.

The children thanked Mrs. Spencer for the lemonade and headed home with their paper airplanes. By the time they reached their own backyard, Violet had been quiet for a long time. She seemed lost in her own thoughts. Jessie could tell something was troubling her.

"Violet?" she asked. "Is anything wrong?"

"I was just thinking about Mrs. Spencer," Violet answered. "Did you notice anything different about her today?"

Jessie thought for a moment. "Well . . . she *did* seem a bit distracted."

"I noticed that, too," said Henry.

Violet sighed. "She just wasn't her usual cheery self."

Just then, Watch flattened his ears and let out a whine. Henry looked up. "What is it, Watch?"

Their little dog tilted his head as if he were listening to something that no one else could hear. A moment later, he ran over to the back fence and began to bark.

"I wonder why Watch is acting so weird," said Benny.

Jessie pulled a dog biscuit from her back pocket. "Come here, Watch!" she shouted, waving the biscuit in the air.

At the sound of Jessie's voice, Watch came running. It wasn't long before his tail was wagging happily as he munched on his treat.

"Well, that did the trick," said Violet.

Benny nodded. "Food always does the trick for me, too."

"We get the hint, Benny." Henry laughed. "Let's have an airplane race, then you can get lunch."

On the count of three, they threw their paper airplanes into the air. Jessie's took a nosedive first, followed by Henry's, and then Violet's. Benny's airplane made it all the way to the fence, and the others let out a cheer.

"Looks like we have a champ!" said Henry.

Benny beamed. "I never thought I'd beat *you* in a race, Henry."

Henry smiled. "Size doesn't matter, Benny. Not when it comes to flying paper airplanes."

"Or finding clues," Benny reminded his brother. "Right?" The others nodded in agreement. The Aldens loved mysteries, and together they'd managed to solve quite a few.

As their dog came running over, Benny hurried off to get their airplanes. Henry knelt down and wrapped his arms around Watch's neck. "Better stay here, Watch," he said. "Airplanes won't fly if they're all chewed up."

A moment later, Benny came running back, shaking his head. He was still shaking his head when they sat cross-legged under the tree. "There's something I don't get," he said.

"What is it, Benny?" Jessie asked.

Benny looked around at them. "I thought there were *four* airplanes in the race."

"That's right," Henry replied. "Couldn't you find them all?"

"Oh, I found them all," Benny was quick to reply. Then he got a funny look on his face. "The problem is, I found too many!"

They all looked over at him in surprise. "What do you mean, Benny?" Violet asked.

Benny set the paper airplanes down, one at a time, on the grass while he counted aloud: "One . . . two . . . three . . . four . . . *five*!"

"That's weird," said Jessie. "How can there be five airplanes?"

"Well . . . " Violet thought for a minute. "Benny *did* make two. Remember?"

"But I've still got the chewed-up one in my pocket," said Benny. And he pulled it out for Violet to see.

"Then one of those airplanes isn't ours," concluded Henry.

Jessie blinked. "How can that be?"

"Maybe Watch made one when we weren't looking," said Henry. He sounded serious, but there was a teasing twinkle in his eye.

Benny looked up at his older brother. "Watch is a smart dog, but not *that* smart!"

Jessie took a closer look at one of the airplanes. Carefully, she unfolded it. As she flattened out the creases, her eyebrows suddenly shot up. "What in the world . . . ?" Her voice trailed off.

Violet moved closer to her sister. "What's wrong, Jessie?"

Jessie didn't answer right away. "It's the strangest thing," she said at last. "There's a . . . a message on this airplane!"

Confused, the other Aldens looked at one another. What kind of message would be on a paper airplane that came from out of nowhere?

CHAPTER 2

The Strange Message

Everyone stared wide-eyed at the message on the airplane. It was printed in thick black ink. "I can't believe it," Violet said in a hushed voice.

"Read it, Jessie," urged Benny.

Jessie tucked her dark hair behind her ears, then read the message out loud:

> "In a bed of pansies,
> A snapdragon lurks;
> In the house of Spencer
> A mystery perks."

"That sure is weird," remarked Henry. "I wonder who wrote it."

Jessie had an answer. "The Tattletale," she said, pointing to the paper. "At least, that's how he—or she—signed the message."

Benny looked confused. "What's a tattle-tale?"

"Somebody who tells secrets," explained Jessie.

"But you're not supposed to tell secrets," Benny said with a frown.

This made Jessie smile a little. Benny was famous for not keeping secrets. "Well, it's not very nice," she said, "if it's somebody else's secrets you're telling."

"But . . . who is it?" Violet wondered. "Who's the Tattletale?"

Henry answered, "That's a good question."

"One thing's for sure," said Benny. "The Tattletale knows we're detectives."

Violet looked over at her younger brother. "Why do you say that, Benny?"

"Well, why else would a message about a mystery come flying into *our* yard?"

"Good point," said Violet.

"That's not all," Jessie put in. "He — or she — knows Mrs. Spencer, too."

Henry suddenly looked around. "Maybe the Tattletale is still close by." He put a finger to his lips, signaling for his brother and sisters to be quiet. "I'll check it out."

"We'll help you," volunteered Benny.

Henry jumped to his feet. So did everyone else. Without wasting another minute, the four Aldens and Watch took a long and careful look around the house and in the neighboring yards. Henry put his hand up to shade his eyes as he glanced up and down the street out front. The only person in sight was Mrs. Turner, who was driving away after visiting with Mrs. McGregor. But the children didn't think there was anything suspicious about Mrs. Turner. She worked at Cooke's Drugstore and was good friends with the Aldens' housekeeper.

"It's almost as if . . ." Jessie stopped in midsentence.

"As if the message came from out of nowhere," finished Benny.

Violet looked around a little nervously. "It does seem that way."

But Henry wasn't having any of that. "We're just too late," he said. "Whoever threw that airplane took off."

As they sat down in the backyard again, Benny thought of something. "I bet that's why Watch was acting weird before."

"You're right," said Henry. "I bet Watch knew somebody was close by. We should've paid more attention."

After Jessie read the message aloud one more time, Violet said, "I wonder what it means about a snapdragon in a bed of pansies." It seemed very odd to her.

"There's no such thing as a dragon," stated Benny. He paused. "Is there?"

"No, there isn't," Jessie assured Benny. "But there *is* such a thing as a snapdragon."

Violet nodded. "A snapdragon's a flower with petals that look like a dragon's face, and — "

"Look at this!" Jessie broke in as something caught her eye. There was a bright pink snapdragon drawn on the other side of the airplane. She held it up for the others to see.

"Oh!" Violet put one hand over her mouth in surprise. "Whoever drew that picture is a wonderful artist," she said. Violet loved to draw and paint. And she was good at it, too.

Henry added up the clues. "The Tattletale is artistic *and* knows we're detectives. Plus, he — or she — knows Mrs. Spencer."

"It's not much to go on," Benny pointed out.

Henry scratched his head. "It's a mystery, that's for sure," he said. "And it's a mystery that landed right in our own backyard!"

CHAPTER 3

A Mystery Perks

"The Aldens!" Mrs. Spencer looked surprised. She stood at the door, wiping her hands on an apron. Her snowy white hair was pulled back into a bun. "Back again! Did you forget something?"

Jessie shook her head. "We didn't forget anything, Mrs. Spencer," she said. "We just . . . wanted to ask you about something."

"If you're not too busy," Violet quickly put in.

"Oh?" Mrs. Spencer looked around at them in surprise.

Jessie said, "This is going to sound a little weird, but — "

"A strange message landed in our backyard!" Benny blurted out before Jessie could finish her sentence.

Henry added, "On a paper airplane."

"A message on a . . . a paper airplane?" The elderly woman looked startled. "I don't believe it." She went into the kitchen and sat down at a table. The Aldens joined her.

"I know it must sound very odd," admitted Violet. "I mean, you were just telling us about your school days, and how you passed messages on paper airplanes. But . . . it really did happen."

"And we were wondering if it has anything to do with you, Mrs. Spencer." Jessie pulled the message from her pocket and passed it across the table.

"Another thing," added Benny. "Do you have any snapdragons in your garden, Mrs. Spencer?"

Mrs. Spencer caught her breath. "Any . . . *what*?"

"Snapdragons."

Benny's words seemed to frighten Mrs. Spencer, and she stared wide-eyed at him. Her eyes grew even bigger when she looked down and read the strange message.

Jessie glanced at Henry. There was no doubt about it. It *was* about Mrs. Spencer. The look in Henry's eye told her he was thinking the same thing.

"Do you have any idea who wrote that message, Mrs. Spencer?" Henry asked.

But their friend didn't answer.

"Mrs. Spencer?" Jessie asked again. "We were wondering if you knew who the Tattletale might be."

Mrs. Spencer still didn't answer. She seemed to be in a daze.

Violet rested a hand on Mrs. Spencer's arm. "If something's wrong," she said softly, "won't you let us help?" She hated to see their friend so upset.

"We're good detectives," Benny couldn't help adding.

"I have no idea who this Tattletale person is," Mrs. Spencer said at last. "How could anyone know about all the . . . the

strange things that have been happening? I haven't breathed a word of it to anyone." She shook her head in disbelief.

"Is it true, then?" Henry wanted to know. "Is there really a mystery?"

Looking pale and shaken, Mrs. Spencer nodded. "You won't be able to make any sense of it, though" she said. "After all, *I* can't make any sense of it, and I knew Milly Manchester all my life."

The children looked at one another in surprise. "Wasn't Milly your friend from school?" Jessie asked.

"Could you tell us more about her?" urged Henry.

"Oh, it happened such a long time ago," Mrs. Spencer told them, a faraway look in her eyes. "Milly and I were just young girls when we spotted that bright pink snap-dragon."

The Aldens inched their chairs closer. They wanted to catch every word.

"You see, somehow it had managed to seed itself right in the middle of my mother's purple pansies." A slow smile spread across the elderly woman's face. "We laughed so hard. We thought that snapdragon was playing a great joke on those pansies, and Milly got out her sketch pad and drew a picture of it." Mrs. Spencer paused. "That was the day she decided to become an artist."

"Because of a snapdragon?" Benny found it hard to believe.

"It made Milly realize that anything's possible," said Mrs. Spencer, smiling over at Benny. "And she never forgot the reason she became an artist. Instead of signing her paintings, she put a bright pink snapdragon somewhere in each one. She said it was the only signature she needed."

"Then Milly really *did* become an artist?" Violet asked.

"A truly gifted one," answered Mrs. Spencer, "even though she never sold a single painting."

"Why didn't she sell any?" Henry wondered.

"Milly simply wasn't interested in fame and fortune." Mrs. Spencer shrugged a little. "Believe me, I always encouraged her to enter her paintings in art shows. There's a contest sponsored every year by the Mona Lisa Gallery here in Greenfield. I told her she'd be a shoo-in to win. I figured if she'd only put her paintings on display, it wouldn't be long before art dealers and collectors were beating a path to her door.

"But Milly didn't want to spend her time like that, promoting her work," Mrs. Spencer went on. "She just wanted to spend her time painting, even if it meant never having any money. And that's exactly how she lived her life — right up until the end." Mrs. Spencer sighed deeply. "I'm afraid my dear friend passed away a few months ago."

"Oh!" Jessie cried. "How sad."

"Milly lived a long and happy life," Mrs. Spencer assured them. "Nobody can ask for more than that."

"Do you have any of Milly's paintings, Mrs. Spencer?" Violet asked. "I'd love to see them."

"I'm afraid you're out of luck, Violet," answered Mrs. Spencer. "I wish you could see her self-portrait. I was especially fond of it, and Milly left it to me in her will. After she died, I tried to find the painting. But it was never found among her possessions."

Henry raised his eyebrows. "That's strange."

"Not as strange as you might think, Henry," Mrs. Spencer told him. "Milly often painted over her finished works. You see, there were times when she was short of cash to buy new canvas. I imagine that's what happened to the self-portrait," she added. "It was always the act of creating that Milly valued, not the finished work."

Benny asked, "But what about her other paintings?"

"Milly left those to her nephew, Jem Manchester. A lot of people thought that was very odd, of course. She didn't always get along with Jem, and he'd never taken any interest in art. But he was the only family Milly had, so she left her paintings to him on one condition."

The Aldens were instantly curious. "What was the condition?"

"That her paintings never be sold," replied Mrs. Spencer. "Milly always felt her nephew was too interested in money for his own good."

"Interested enough to sell the paintings?" Violet asked in surprise.

"It's hard to say. But I guess Milly wasn't taking any chances. Jem's not a bad person, but he does place too much importance on money. I think Milly was hoping her paintings would change that. Her real gift to him was an opportunity to appreciate art. Of course, it's too late for that now."

"Too late?" Violet looked puzzled.

Mrs. Spencer nodded. "Jem took the paintings up north to his cabin. Somehow a fire started, and all of Milly's paintings were destroyed."

"Oh, no!" Violet cried, horrified.

For a few moments, no one spoke. Then Mrs. Spencer leaned closer, as if she were about to share a secret. "It was a few weeks after the fire that strange things started happening." The elderly woman pushed her chair back. "There's something I must show you." And she led the way outside.

Curious, the children followed Mrs. Spencer out to a small garden edged with flowers.

"It's really beautiful out here," Violet said admiringly.

"Thank you, Violet." Mrs. Spencer sounded pleased. "Gardening is a great hobby of mine. And my daughter, Rachel, comes over to help with the weeding now and again."

Jessie suddenly gasped. "Look!"

The other Aldens looked in the direction she was pointing. "Oh, my goodness!" cried Violet. "That's . . . that's — "

"Yes, it is," Mrs. Spencer cut in, nodding. "It's a snapdragon."

Sure enough, a bright pink snapdragon was growing in the very middle of a bed of purple pansies. The four Aldens stared at it in disbelief. Finally Henry gave a low whistle. "Wow," he said, astonished. "It happened again!"

Mrs. Spencer shivered a little. "It's the strangest thing."

Benny squatted down next to the flower bed. "It's just like before, Mrs. Spencer. Just like when you and Milly found that snapdragon in your mother's pansy bed."

"But . . . how did it get there?" Violet wanted to know.

Mrs. Spencer was shaking her head. "I have no idea. Oh, I thought it was just a coincidence at first." She took a deep breath to steady her voice. "But then . . . something else happened."

"What?" asked Benny, his eyes huge.

"Last week I was reading in the park," she told them. "I got up for a moment to feed bread crumbs to the birds and left my book on the bench. When I sat down again, I found something stuck between the pages."

The children waited breathlessly while Mrs. Spencer fished around in the pocket of her apron. Benny couldn't stand the suspense. "What did you find?"

Mrs. Spencer held up a bookmark with a bright pink snapdragon painted on it.

"Ohhhh," Violet breathed.

They all moved closer for a better look. "I don't understand," Henry said, puzzled. "How could a bookmark suddenly appear like that inside your book?"

Jessie added, "Did you notice anyone nearby?"

"I looked around, but I didn't see any-one."

"Are you sure?" Henry looked uncertain. Mrs. Spencer nodded. "Quite sure, Henry."

"I bet it came from out of nowhere," offered Benny. "Just like the paper airplane."

"There must be an explanation for it," insisted Henry. "We just have to figure out what it is." Then he noticed something half hidden in the long grass. "Look at this," he said. He bent down and picked up a shiny gold hair clip.

"What sharp eyes!" exclaimed Mrs. Spencer. "No wonder you children are such good detectives."

"Is it yours, Mrs. Spencer?" Henry wondered, holding it out to her.

"No, it isn't, Henry." She examined it

closely, then handed it back to him. "I've never seen it before."

"Could it belong to your daughter?" suggested Jessie.

Mrs. Spencer shook her head. "Rachel keeps her hair very short. She'd have no use for hair clips."

Henry slipped it into his pocket. He wasn't sure, but he thought it might be a clue.

As the Aldens followed Mrs. Spencer back to the house, Jessie noted, "That makes two strange things that have happened: the snapdragon growing in the garden, and the bookmark appearing inside the book."

Mrs. Spencer glanced back at them. "*Three* strange things," she corrected. "There's something I haven't shown you yet."

The Aldens looked at one another. Everything was becoming more and more mysterious.

CHAPTER 4

The Key to a Rhyme

As the Aldens settled around the table again, Mrs. Spencer opened a kitchen drawer. She pulled out a white envelope. "I found this in my mailbox this morning," she told them in a quiet voice.

"What is it, Mrs. Spencer?" Violet couldn't help asking. She was almost afraid to hear the answer.

Mrs. Spencer sat down. "Maybe you should see for yourself." She pushed the envelope across the table.

Violet hesitated. Then, with a slow nod,

she opened the envelope and unfolded a sheet of white paper. Her eyes widened. "Oh!" she gasped.

"Is anything wrong, Violet?" inquired Henry.

"What is it?" asked Jessie at the same time.

Violet's eyebrows drew together in a frown. "I don't know what it is," she told them. "It's impossible to read."

Violet passed the note to Henry. Henry passed it to Benny. Then Benny passed it to Jessie. But nobody could make any sense of it.

"Violet's right," Jessie said, after turning the note upside down. "It's impossible to read."

Henry said, "It must be written in some kind of code."

"Look on the other side, Jessie," suggested Mrs. Spencer. "There's a message on the back that isn't in code."

Jessie flipped the paper over. It was a note from the Tattletale:

She is guarded in Greenfield
By night and by day
And the smile on her lips
Never does go away
The smile is more famous
Than any in history
And behind it there lurks
A mysterious mystery

"To solve this code
Go back in time;
Leonardo da Vinci
Holds the key to a rhyme."

Benny made a face as Jessie read it aloud. "Who's Leonardo da . . . da — "

"Da Vinci," finished Mrs. Spencer. "He was an artist who lived a long time ago."

The Aldens looked at one another but didn't say anything. They didn't have to. They were all thinking the same thing. How could an artist who lived a long time ago help them break the code?

"He was one of Milly's favorite artists," said Mrs. Spencer. Then she lowered her voice to a whisper. "Sometimes I get the feeling it's Milly herself doing all these strange things."

"What do you mean, Mrs. Spencer?" Benny's eyes were huge.

Mrs. Spencer shrugged a little. "I can't help wondering if she's trying to tell me something."

Violet felt an icy chill go through her.

Was Benny right about the paper airplane coming from out of nowhere? Was the ghost of Milly Manchester responsible for everything that had happened?

Jessie spoke up. "You don't really believe that, do you, Mrs. Spencer?" she asked.

"I don't know what to believe," Mrs. Spencer answered. Then she gave her head a shake and laughed. "I'm sure I'm getting all worked up about nothing. This is probably just somebody's idea of a joke. Nothing more than that."

"Well, if it's a joke, it's not a very funny one." Henry frowned. "But I don't think we should jump to any conclusions until we do some investigating."

Mrs. Spencer nodded. "That's a good suggestion, Henry."

"Mrs. Spencer, do you mind if we take this message with us?" Jessie asked. "We might be able to break the code."

Mrs. Spencer thought this was a good idea. As Jessie tucked the coded message into her pocket, Henry and Violet looked at each other and smiled. They could always count on Jessie to think of everything.

On the way home, Benny asked the other Aldens a question. "Do you think it's true?"

"What do you mean, Benny?" Jessie asked, as they stopped to wait for a light to change.

"Do you think Milly's doing everything?"

"No." Henry shook his head firmly. "The Tattletale is *not* the ghost of Milly Manchester, Benny." But the youngest Alden didn't look convinced.

That evening at dinner, the children told their grandfather everything that had happened. Jessie finished by saying, "The problem is, we don't have any idea how we're going to solve this mystery."

James Alden finished helping himself to some of Mrs. McGregor's delicious meat loaf. Then he passed the platter to Henry. He looked at his eldest granddaughter. "Unless I miss my guess," he said with a chuckle, "it won't be long until you think of something."

Benny scooped mashed potatoes onto his plate. "Leonardo holds the key."

Grandfather looked over at his youngest grandson. "Leonardo?"

"Leonardo da Vinci," replied Benny. "He was an artist."

"A brilliant artist." Grandfather nodded. "But that's not all. He was also an inventor. In fact, Leonardo da Vinci was probably the greatest genius who ever lived."

The children looked at their grandfather in surprise. "What kind of things did he invent?" Benny wanted to know.

Taking a bite of his meat loaf, Grandfather chewed thoughtfully. "As I recall, he drew designs for diving equipment and a submarine. Even a helicopter and a parachute."

Violet looked puzzled. "But . . . I thought Leonardo da Vinci lived a long time ago."

"He did," Grandfather told her. "Long before the days of flying machines. That's why his ideas are so amazing."

"But I don't get it," said Benny, putting his fork down. "How can he give us the key to a rhyme if he lived in the olden days?"

Henry said, "I think we should find out more about Leonardo da Vinci."

"How will we find out?" asked Benny.

Jessie thought about this. "We can go to the library. We should be able to find lots of information about a genius." And the others agreed.

Right after breakfast the next morning, the Aldens set off on their bikes for the Greenfield Public Library.

"Do you think this is somebody's idea of a joke?" Jessie asked.

Violet looked at her sister. "Oh, Jessie!" she gasped. "Do you really think it's possible?"

"I don't want to think anyone would do something like that, Violet," said Jessie. "But we have to consider everything."

"I have a hunch there's more to it than that," Henry insisted. "After all, the Tattletale went to a lot of trouble making up codes and clues."

"I hope we can figure out why he — or

she — went to so much trouble," Violet said as they slowed to a stop outside the library. She propped her bike against a tree. So did the others.

Inside the library, Henry said, "Let's start by checking the computer catalog." He led the way to a long table with a row of computers on it.

The others gathered around while Henry sat down in front of a computer. His fingers tapped against the keyboard as he searched for any books about Leonardo da Vinci. Before long, a list of titles appeared on the screen. Jessie wrote the Dewey decimal numbers on a piece of paper, then they all hurried off to search the shelves.

When their arms were full, the children headed for an empty table by the window. They sat down with their books piled high in front of them.

"How nice to see the Aldens again!" said a voice behind them, and the children turned around in surprise. An attractive young woman with reddish brown hair smiled at them.

"Hi, Janice!" said Jessie, returning the young woman's friendly smile. The children were regular visitors to the library and often ran into Janice Allen.

"I'm impressed," said Janice, noticing all the books in front of them. "What's all this about?" She took a closer look at the titles. "Oh, you're reading about Leonardo da Vinci! We were just studying about him in school." Working at the library was Janice's part-time job while she went to college.

"Do you know a lot about art, Janice?" Violet wondered.

"I know a little about art history," said Janice. Then her smile faded and she sighed. "But when it comes to drawing, I have no talent whatsoever." She noticed someone waiting by the information desk and hurried away.

The Aldens wasted no time getting started. Jessie helped Benny with the harder words. Before long, Henry came across a drawing in red chalk. He turned the book around so the others could see.

"It's a self-portrait of Leonardo da Vinci,"

he said, as they all stared in fascination at the drawing of an elderly man with long hair and a long beard.

"What's a self-portrait?" Benny wanted to know.

"That just means Leonardo drew a picture of himself," explained Jessie.

Violet had found something interesting, too. "This is the *Mona Lisa*." She showed them a painting of a dark-haired woman with a gentle smile. "It's the most famous painting in the world. But Leonardo da Vinci didn't even sign it."

"Just like Milly Manchester," whispered Benny. "She never signed her paintings, either."

After a moment's thought, Jessie said, "That's interesting, but . . . it doesn't help us decode the message."

"That's true," admitted Henry. "I guess we'll just have to look harder." And the others nodded.

A few hours later, Benny finally slumped in his chair, his hands on his cheeks. "We're getting nowhere," he groaned, looking defeated.

Henry glanced up from his book. "Don't be so sure! Listen to this: 'Leonardo da Vinci was afraid his ideas would be stolen, so he wrote his notes in codes and in mirror writing.' "

Benny straightened up. "Wow, Leonardo da Vinci liked mysteries, too! But . . . what's mirror writing?"

"It's writing that's backward," explained Henry. "But if you hold it in front of a mirror, you can read it."

"Do you think the code is mirror writing?" asked Violet.

Jessie fished the message from her pocket. After studying it carefully, she had to admit it was possible. "It just might be."

"There's only one way to find out," said Benny excitedly. "Right, Henry?"

"Right!" Henry sounded just as excited as Benny. "We can use the rearview mirror on my bike."

After returning their library books to be reshelved, the Aldens hurried outside. Benny hopped up and down impatiently as

Jessie held the message up to Henry's rear-view mirror.

"Can you read it, Jessie?" He wanted to know. "Is it mirror writing?"

With a nod, Jessie read the message aloud.

> *"She is guarded in Greenfield*
> *By night and by day*
> *And the smile on her lips*
> *Never does go away*
> *The smile is more famous*
> *Than any in history*
> *And behind it there lurks*
> *A snapdragon mystery."*

"All right!" cried Benny. "Now we're getting somewhere!"

Violet didn't look so sure. "But . . . what does it mean?"

"Beats me," said Henry.

Benny grinned. "We're good detectives," he reminded them. "We'll figure it out."

"I hope so, Benny," said Henry. "I hope so."

CHAPTER 5

A Warning

"Solving mysteries is hard work," Benny said as they wheeled their bikes back onto the road. "But it's fun, too," he quickly added.

"That's for sure!" Jessie said. And the others agreed. The Aldens were never happier than when they were figuring out clues.

Henry looked at his wristwatch. "It's almost lunchtime. Why don't we get something to eat at Cooke's Drugstore."

Benny was grinning from ear to ear. "That's a great idea!"

It wasn't long before they were sitting at the long lunch counter of the drugstore, studying the menus.

"Aaah, my favorite customers!" Mrs. Turner greeted the children with a big smile. Her gray hair was pinned back from her round face. "What'll it be today?"

Henry ordered a ham sandwich, coleslaw, and a cola. Jessie had a bacon and tomato sandwich and milk, and Violet ordered a grilled cheese sandwich and a strawberry milk shake. Benny decided on a hamburger, french fries, a chocolate sundae with extra sprinkles, and milk.

"Benny, you eat like a bird," Mrs. Turner teased good-naturedly. "And I don't mean that kind of bird!"

The children looked at Mrs. Turner, then in the direction she was pointing. Through the big plate-glass window, they could see a small pigeon on the top of the minuteman statue. They couldn't help laughing at Josiah Wade. The Revolutionary War hero was standing in the middle of Town Square with his musket at his side — and a pigeon on his head!

"No, you don't eat like a pigeon, Benny," Mrs. Turner went on. "I was thinking more of those big prehistoric birds."

Benny grinned. "I wonder if they liked extra sprinkles, too," he said, making them all laugh.

While they waited for their food, the Aldens turned their attention to the mystery. "I wish we knew more about the Tattletale," said Jessie. "I can't stop wondering who it is."

"At least we have another clue," put in Henry.

The others looked surprised to hear this. "We do?"

"Sure." Henry nodded. "The Tattletale must be somebody who knows a lot about art history."

Nodding, Violet said, "That's true. How else would he — or she — know that Leonardo da Vinci wrote his notes in codes and mirror writing?"

Benny took a spin on his red-leather stool. "Leonardo really *did* have the key to a rhyme! I can't wait to tell Mrs. Spencer all about it."

"We'll do that right after lunch," Henry said. "And then we can try to figure out what the message means."

As soon as they finished eating, the Aldens biked over to Mrs. Spencer's. Just as they were turning into the driveway, Jessie looked up and saw the elderly woman waving to them from an upstairs window. She was motioning for the children to come in.

After parking their bikes, the Aldens hurried up the front walk. Benny raced ahead of the others. When he stepped inside, his eyebrows shot up in surprise. A woman with short sandy-colored hair was sitting in the living room, flipping through a photograph album.

When the screen door clicked shut, the woman suddenly jumped. She closed the photograph album with a sudden bang, then tossed it quickly onto the coffee table. It was almost as though she'd been caught doing something she shouldn't.

Just as the other Aldens came inside, the woman spotted Benny standing in the doorway. Leaping to her feet, she snapped, "How dare you come in without knocking!"

Benny's face turned bright red. "I'm sorry," he said in a small voice, taking a step back.

Henry was quickly at his brother's side. "We thought Mrs. Spencer wanted us to — " he began.

The woman cut in, "Whatever you're selling, my mother isn't interested."

"You must be Rachel," said Jessie, smiling a little. "We're the Aldens. I'm Jessie. And this is my sister, Violet, and my brothers, Henry and Benny."

"And we're not here to sell anything," Henry assured her.

Violet put in, "Mrs. Spencer's a good friend of ours."

"Well, isn't it just wonderful to meet the Aldens!" Rachel responded, though it was clear from her voice that she didn't think it was wonderful at all. "My mother told me what's been going on, you know," she said, coming out into the hallway. "And I don't like it. Not one little bit!" She gave the children a hard look.

Henry and Jessie turned to each other in disbelief. Why was Rachel so angry?

"You'd better stop this little game of yours. I'm warning you, you'll be sorry if you don't!" And with that, Mrs. Spencer's daughter hurried out the door.

When she was gone, Henry shook his head in astonishment. "What was that all about?"

"I thought we were supposed to come right in." Benny took a deep breath.

Jessie put an arm around her little brother. "Don't worry, Benny," she said, trying to comfort him. "You didn't do anything wrong."

"Did I just hear Rachel leave?" Mrs. Spencer asked as she came down the stairs. When the children nodded, she said, "Oh, dear. I was hoping we could all have a nice visit together."

"I don't think Rachel likes us very much." Benny still felt upset.

"I'm sure she likes you just fine, Benny," Mrs. Spencer assured him. "Rachel has a good heart, but sometimes she gets a bit grumpy. You mustn't let it bother you. She's been a bit worried about money lately. She's a real estate agent, and things are slow for her at work right now. I keep telling her to go into nursing. Rachel always wanted to become a nurse, you know. But she says she can't afford to go back to school. The truth is, she *could* afford it if she'd move back home with me for a while. But she insists she doesn't want to get in the way. And she thinks she's too old to go back to school."

"That's a shame," said Jessie, softening a little toward Rachel.

Mrs. Spencer suddenly changed the subject. "I'm glad you stopped by," she said. "I have something to show you." Then she led the way into the living room.

"You mentioned you wanted to see one of Milly's paintings, Violet." Mrs. Spencer made herself comfortable on the sofa. "I remembered a picture I'd taken in Milly's backyard." She reached for the photograph album. Everyone gathered around as she turned the pages one by one.

"Here it is." Mrs. Spencer put her finger under a snapshot of an elderly woman sitting at an easel, her hair hanging down her back in one long silver braid. There was a young woman standing nearby. "You can see what Milly's painting. It's the self-portrait I was telling you about."

Violet looked closely at the photograph. "Oh, she really *was* a wonderful artist!" she said, admiringly.

Benny pointed to the young woman in the photograph. "Who's that?" he asked.

The other Aldens had been wondering about her, too. The young woman was wearing jeans and a white T-shirt, and her blond hair was pulled back into a ponytail.

"Oh, that's Peg," Mrs. Spencer answered. "She was a promising young artist Milly'd taken under her wing. Milly was always encouraging her to develop a style of her own. But Peg was too eager to make a name for herself in the art world. She liked to imi-

tate the latest up-and-coming artists. Milly, on the other hand, was one of a kind." Mrs. Spencer suddenly sighed. "Oh, I do miss her!"

None of the Aldens liked to hear the sadness in Mrs. Spencer's voice. Violet was trying to find something cheery to say when Jessie spoke up.

"You won't believe this, but we figured out the coded message!"

Mrs. Spencer looked surprised — and pleased.

After telling Mrs. Spencer about their visit to the library, Jessie read the rhyme they'd decoded out loud.

"It doesn't make any sense to us," finished Violet.

Mrs. Spencer threw up her hands. "I'm afraid it doesn't make any sense to me, either."

The Aldens looked at one another. They were each thinking the same thing: How were they going to solve such a strange mystery?

CHAPTER 6

Keep Smiling!

It rained in Greenfield for the next few days, and the children spent their time inside, puzzling over the strange rhyme. They thought and thought, but they still couldn't come up with any answers.

"I have an idea," Violet said when the sun finally came out. "Let's pack a picnic lunch and eat in the park."

The others agreed. "We could use a break," said Henry.

"I love picnics!" Benny got out the peanut butter and jelly.

"Maybe we should stop at Mrs. Spencer's on the way," Jessie suggested. She got out the bread, cold cuts, lettuce, and mustard.

But Violet wasn't so sure this was a good idea. "We're not having much luck with the mystery. Mrs. Spencer will be so disappointed."

"You're right, Violet," Jessie said after a moment's thought. "Let's wait until we have good news."

Benny looked relieved. "I didn't want to go over there, anyway. Rachel wasn't very nice to us."

"I wonder why she was acting so weird," Henry said.

"Things are slow for her at work right now," Jessie reminded them.

Benny filled a thermos with water for Watch. "She said we'd be sorry if we keep playing games," he said in a worried tone of voice. "I wonder what she meant."

"I don't know," Jessie said. "But I think we should concentrate on one mystery at a time."

After cleaning up the kitchen, the children loaded their picnic lunch into Jessie's backpack and set off for the park. Henry held Watch's leash as they pedaled along. They were careful not to go too fast so that Watch could keep up with them.

At the park, Jessie spread the old blanket on the grass, and the children sat cross-legged on it. Watch curled up close to Benny, keeping an eye on the sandwiches. Watch loved peanut butter.

"I don't get it," said Benny. He held out his special cup as Violet poured the lemonade. It was the cracked pink cup he had found when they were living in the boxcar.

"What don't you get, Benny?" Jessie looked over at her little brother as she unwrapped a ham sandwich.

Benny looked puzzled. "How can anyone smile *all* the time? My face would get sore from all that smiling."

"Maybe it's a snapshot of someone smiling," Henry said thoughtfully as Jessie handed him a sandwich.

"Or a painting," Violet was quick to add.

Jessie recited the first few lines of the rhyme. " 'She is guarded in Greenfield/ By night and by day,/ And the smile on her lips/ Never does go away.' "

"Don't forget the rest of it," put in Benny. " 'The smile is more famous/ Than any in history,/ And behind it there lurks/ A snapdragon mystery.' " The Aldens had read the rhyme so many times, they knew it by heart.

No one said anything for a while. They were all completely baffled by the strange rhyme. After lunch, they put all thoughts of the mystery aside as they played a friendly game of touch football, with Watch running all around them in circles. When they sat down to catch their breath, Watch slurped up his water noisily.

"An ice-cream cone would sure hit the spot right now," Benny hinted.

Henry took out his money and counted the change. "You're in luck, Benny. Looks like I have enough for ice cream."

After cleaning up and making sure they

hadn't left any litter, they wheeled their bikes back onto the road and headed for Cooke's Drugstore.

"This was a good idea, Benny," Jessie said, as she leaned against the minuteman statue in the middle of Town Square. She licked a drop of strawberry ice cream from the back of her hand.

Benny grinned. "I told you it would hit the spot! Right, Watch?"

Watch looked up and barked as if in agreement. Then he went back to chewing on his special doggy treat.

Violet put a hand up to shade her eyes. "Isn't that Janice from the library?" Everyone turned to look at the young woman coming toward them across the brick-paved square.

"Hi, kids!" Janice greeted them with a warm smile. She was wearing a pale green skirt and matching blouse. "Enjoying the sunshine?" she asked them.

"We sure are," said Jessie. She smiled back at Janice.

"I just wish I could enjoy it, too." Janice

sighed as she gazed up at the clear blue sky. "But I'm scheduled to work at the library all afternoon and then tonight at my other job."

"You have *two* jobs?" Violet asked in surprise.

Then Henry added, "That must be hard."

"It's the only way I can afford to go to college," said Janice. "But I like my jobs," she added. "Especially the one at the Mona Lisa Gallery." The children followed her gaze to the gallery, tucked between stores on one side of Town Square. A sign hung out front with a picture of the *Mona Lisa* on it.

"The art critics had a sneak preview of the latest exhibit," she went on, "and they gave Peg's — I mean Margaret's — paintings rave reviews. Of course, that means it'll be crowded at the gallery this evening. But I don't mind. It's always so exciting when there's a new exhibit."

Violet looked puzzled. "Who's Margaret?"

"Margaret Longford," answered Janice.

"Peg's her nickname. I know her from school, but . . . I had no idea she was such a brilliant artist. She won the contest this year. The one sponsored by the gallery."

"Milly Manchester could have won that contest," put in Benny. "She could've won just like that!" He snapped his fingers.

Janice looked over at the Aldens in surprise. "It's funny, I just heard that name recently. Did you know Milly Manchester?"

"No." Henry shook his head. "But a good friend of ours did."

"And so did the Tattletale," added Benny, not noticing Jessie's warning look.

"Who?"

Jessie quickly changed the subject. "Benny, I think you have more chocolate ice cream on your face than in your mouth," she said, handing him a napkin.

Janice looked down at her wristwatch. "I'm going to be late if I don't hurry. See you later," she said, dashing away. She turned and waved back to them. " 'Bye, kids! 'Bye, Watch!"

Jessie stared after her, puzzled. Nobody

had mentioned Watch's name. How did Janice know it? Jessie couldn't shake the feeling that something wasn't quite right. She was trying to sort out her thoughts when Benny suddenly spoke up.

"I bet Josiah Wade's happier today," he observed. The youngest Alden was gazing up at the statue of the Revolutionary War hero.

"What do you mean, Benny?" Henry wanted to know.

"I don't think he liked it before," said Benny. "When he was standing guard with a pigeon on his head, I mean."

Violet giggled. "He *did* look funny. Didn't he, Benny?"

Benny didn't answer. His mouth had suddenly dropped open.

"Benny, are you okay?" asked Violet.

"It's . . . it's Josiah!" Benny was pointing up at the minuteman.

The others looked from Benny to the statue and back again. "What about him?" Henry asked.

Benny was so excited, he was hopping on

one foot. "Remember how the rhyme begins? 'She is guarded in Greenfield/ By night and by day.' "

Jessie's eyes widened as she caught Benny's meaning. "Josiah Wade is standing *guard*!"

"And that means—" began Henry.

"That the lady with the famous smile must be close by!" finished Violet.

The Aldens let out a cheer.

"That was good detective work, Benny," praised Violet.

Benny beamed. "Thanks."

The Aldens let their eyes wander around Town Square. Their gaze took in the parking lot on one side of the square, the shops and businesses that lined two sides, and the Town Hall that occupied the fourth side.

"Let's check out the stores," Henry suggested.

Jessie nodded. "Good idea."

The children finished up the last of their cones, then headed across the brick pavement. Henry looped Watch's leash around his wrist so he couldn't pull away. He didn't want him to get lost in the crowd of shoppers.

Taking turns waiting outside with Watch, they went into every store along one side of the square. Then they went into every store along the other side of the square. When they were finished, though, they were still no closer to solving the mystery.

The children turned to one another in dismay. They had been so sure they were on the right track.

As they headed toward the lot where their bikes were parked, Benny said, "Maybe Mrs. Turner's the lady with the smile."

"Mrs. Turner *is* famous for her friendly smile, Benny," admitted Jessie. "But I don't think she has the most famous smile in history."

Violet drew in her breath as a sudden thought came to her. She stopped so quickly that Henry almost ran right into her. "Of course!" she cried. She gave her forehead a smack with the palm of her hand. "Why didn't I think of that before?"

"What's the matter, Violet?" Jessie asked her in alarm.

"It's the *Mona Lisa!*" Violet's eyes were shining as she turned to her sister and brothers. "She's the one with the most famous smile in history!"

Jessie raised her eyebrows in surprise. "You mean that painting by Leonardo da Vinci?"

"Yes!" cried Violet, her voice excited.

Jessie looked puzzled. So did Benny and Henry.

"What makes you so sure, Violet?" Henry wanted to know.

"Remember how her lips curl up just a little? Nobody knows why she's smiling like that. That's what makes her smile so mysterious."

"But that painting's in a museum far away, Violet," Benny pointed out. "Josiah Wade isn't guarding it."

Henry suddenly snapped his fingers. "Wait a minute!"

They all turned to look at Henry.

"Josiah Wade *is* guarding the Mona Lisa

Gallery," he said. "And there's even a picture of the *Mona Lisa* on the sign out front."

"That's right!" Jessie cried in surprise. "We didn't go inside because it was — "

"Closed," finished Benny, suddenly remembering.

"Then that's where the Tattletale's clues are leading us," Jessie concluded, looking back over her shoulder toward the Mona Lisa Gallery.

"But why?" Benny wanted to know.

It was a good question. But none of them had the answer.

CHAPTER 7

The Invitation

"It was the *Mona Lisa*," Henry told Grandfather that evening at dinner. "She's the lady with the famous smile."

"And thanks to Violet," added Jessie, helping herself to the roasted potatoes, "we finally figured it out."

Benny, who was pouring gravy onto his roast beef, suddenly looked up. "I helped, too," he reminded them.

"You sure did." Henry nodded. "You figured out that Josiah Wade was the one standing guard."

Violet lifted green beans onto her plate. "We stopped in to tell Mrs. Spencer about it. But she wasn't home."

"What I can't understand," put in Henry, "is what the Mona Lisa Gallery has to do with a snapdragon mystery."

"Milly Manchester's the key," said Benny. "I just know it."

The others had to admit Benny was right. All the clues had something to do with Milly.

Jessie started adding everything up on her fingers. "There's the message on the paper airplane. Didn't Milly and Mrs. Spencer pass messages like that in school? And how about the snapdragon in Mrs. Spencer's pansy bed? Milly became an artist because of a snapdragon."

"She even put them in her paintings," Benny reminded them.

"Don't forget about Leonardo da Vinci," put in Violet. "He was Milly's favorite artist."

"Even the Mona Lisa Gallery has a connection," Henry pointed out. "Mrs. Spencer always wanted Milly to enter their contest."

Jessie nodded. "I bet that's where we'll find the missing piece of this puzzle."

"Speaking of the gallery," said Grandfather, as he reached into his pocket, "I have something you might find interesting." He pulled out a square white envelope and handed it to Violet.

Curious, Violet put down her fork and opened the flap of the envelope. Pulling out a white card, she read aloud the words in fancy gold script: " 'To James Alden and Guests, You are invited to the opening-night exhibit of works by Margaret Longford, winner of the annual art contest sponsored by the gallery. Mona Lisa Gallery. Greenfield Town Square.' "

"I'm on the gallery's mailing list," explained Grandfather.

"Oh, Grandfather!" cried Violet. "That's tonight! Are you going?"

"Well, I just might," said Grandfather, his eyes twinkling. "If I have some company, that is."

Violet clasped her hands together. "It

would be wonderful to go to an art show."

"And we can look for clues while we're there!" Benny was so excited, he was bouncing in his seat.

James Alden smiled at the children's eager faces. "I'm not sure you'll get a chance to do much detective work," he warned them. "I have a hunch the gallery will be packed to the rafters tonight. From what Edmund tells me, Margaret Longford's paintings have caused quite a sensation."

Henry lifted an eyebrow. "Edmund?"

"Edmund Rondale's the owner of the Mona Lisa Gallery," Grandfather told Henry. "He takes great pride in discovering new artists."

"Oh, I can't wait to go!" cried Violet. She sounded very excited.

Soon enough, the children were coming down the stairs, ready for their night out. Jessie was wearing a pale pink skirt and a white blouse. Violet had a lavender ribbon in her hair that matched her frilly lavender dress. Benny had changed into a gray blazer and navy trousers. And Henry was wearing a maroon blazer and gray trousers.

"My, what a fine-looking group!" said Mrs. McGregor, smiling fondly at the children.

"We wanted to look especially nice for the art show." Benny gave his neatly combed hair a little pat.

James Alden was adjusting his tie in the hall mirror. "No one will ever guess you're on the trail of a mystery, Benny." He smiled over at his youngest grandson.

"No one except the Tattletale!" Benny said.

"I wonder if the Tattletale will be there tonight," Violet said, climbing into Grandfather's station wagon.

"It's hard to say." Henry, who was sitting up front beside Grandfather, looked over his shoulder. "But we'll keep an eye out for anything suspicious."

As they pulled into the busy parking lot, Jessie said, "You were right, Grandfather. I think everyone in Greenfield is headed for the art show."

Violet looked around uneasily at all the smartly dressed people making a beeline for the Mona Lisa Gallery. She was shy, and meeting new people often made her nervous. As they crossed the square, she slowed her step.

Grandfather put a comforting arm around his youngest granddaughter. "It'll be worth braving the crowds," he assured her. "Edmund says Margaret Longford's paintings are the finest work by a new artist that he's ever seen."

Violet smiled up at her grandfather and quickened her pace. She *was* eager to see Margaret's paintings.

As they entered the gallery, a tall man in a tuxedo rushed over. "James! I was hoping you could make it." He put out his hand.

"I always enjoy coming to your gallery, Edmund," said Grandfather, shaking hands. He introduced the children to the owner of the Mona Lisa Gallery.

"It's nice to meet you, Mr. Rondale," Henry said politely, speaking for them all.

"Please call me Edmund. Everyone around here does."

Benny glanced over at all the guests crowded around the paintings. He saw one familiar face. It was Mrs. Turner. When the waitress spotted Benny, she smiled and waved her hand. Benny waved, too.

Violet followed Benny's gaze. "I didn't know Mrs. Turner liked art," she said in surprise.

"I didn't, either," said Jessie. "But I guess everybody wants to see Margaret Longford's work."

"Will all those people buy paintings?" Benny wanted to know.

Edmund laughed. "I wouldn't be surprised, Benny. Everybody's very impressed with this year's contest winner." He lowered his voice, leaning closer. "The art world's just buzzing. It won't be long before Margaret Longford makes quite a name for herself."

"If the paintings are half as good as you say, Edmund," responded Grandfather, "I just might buy one myself."

"The paintings in this room will be on exhibit all week," Edmund told Grandfather. "But if anything strikes your fancy, I'll tag it and you can pick it up when the show's over. Of course, we have a number of Margaret's canvasses in the back room that haven't been framed yet. If you decide to purchase one of those, you can take it away with you tonight. Then you can get it framed later."

Grandfather nodded. "I'll keep that in mind."

"We have our usual assortment of sandwiches and pastries, of course," Edmund went on. He gestured to a long table where Janice Allen was busy pouring coffee for the guests. "Please help yourselves." With that, the gallery owner hurried away.

"I can't wait to get a close look at the paintings," Violet said, feeling less shy now.

Jessie nodded. "I'm curious to see them, too." Then she noticed Benny eyeing the refreshment table. She guessed what was coming next. "You want something to eat. Right, Benny?"

"I am getting kind of hungry," Benny

said, to no one's surprise. He looked at his grandfather expectantly. "Is it all right, Grandfather?"

James Alden chuckled. "Edmund said to help yourselves."

Henry knew there was no stopping his little brother. "Come on, Benny," he said, and led the way over to the table in the corner.

While Grandfather mingled with the other guests, Violet and Jessie threaded their way through the crowds to see the paintings. Violet caught her breath as she gazed at a canvas splashed with color. "Oh, how beautiful!" she breathed.

Jessie nodded. "No wonder everyone's so impressed."

As they moved from painting to painting, Jessie and Violet kept a sharp eye out for any clues. Although they didn't mean to eavesdrop, they couldn't help overhearing what people were saying about Margaret Longford's work.

"Just look at the bold swirls of the brushstroke!"

"Magnificent!"

"This artist is one of a kind."

Jessie smiled over at her sister. "One day your paintings will be hanging here, Violet."

"Do you really think so?" Violet asked her, hopefully.

Before Jessie had a chance to answer, Henry and Benny came rushing up. "Did you find anything suspicious?" Benny wanted to know. He swallowed a bite of his egg sandwich.

"Not a thing." Jessie shook her head. "Grandfather was right. It's hard to look for clues when it's so crowded."

Violet looked over at Henry and Benny. "Did you strike out, too?"

"Not exactly. We came across something kind of . . . weird," Henry said, and Benny nodded in agreement.

Full of curiosity, Jessie and Violet quickly followed Henry and Benny, weaving their way around the guests. On the far side of the room, Henry pointed to the wall, where a sheet of paper had been pinned.

"Everybody who entered the contest is on that list," he said. "And guess who got an honorable mention?"

"Oh!" exclaimed Violet, her eyes widening when Henry placed his finger under Janice Allen's name. "But . . . Janice told us she couldn't draw. Remember?"

Benny nodded. "I wonder why she lied to us."

"That's what I'd like to know," said Henry. "It seems kind of strange. Don't you think, Jessie?"

Jessie didn't answer. She was thinking hard. Suddenly she said, "There's something else that's strange. When Janice said good-bye to Watch today, she called him by name. What I can't figure out is how she even *knew* Watch's name. I'm sure we never told her."

Henry, Violet, and Benny had thought nothing of it. But now they wondered about it, too.

"We always leave Watch at home when we go to the library," Henry commented.

Benny nodded. "Dogs aren't allowed in the Greenfield Public Library."

"Maybe somebody else told her about Watch," Violet offered.

Benny thought this was possible. "Watch *is* a very nice dog. Everybody in Greenfield likes him. I bet they talk about him all the time."

"Or . . ." said Jessie, "maybe Janice was there the day the paper airplane flew into our yard. Maybe she heard us calling Watch."

Slowly, the others understood Jessie's meaning.

"You think Janice might be the Tattletale?" Violet asked in surprise.

Still glancing at the list, Jessie nodded. "It's possible. She *has* been studying art history in school," she pointed out.

"If Janice lied when she said she couldn't draw," Henry reasoned, "maybe she was trying to throw us off the track. So we wouldn't suspect her of being the Tattletale, I mean."

Violet looked confused. "But why would Janice leave a trail of clues for us to follow?"

"One thing's for sure," said Benny. "Now we have *two* Tattletale suspects." When he saw their puzzled looks, he added, "Janice Allen and the ghost of Milly Manchester."

Henry looked as if he wanted to argue with Benny, but there was no time. Grandfather was waving them over. James Alden was deep in conversation with Edmund and an attractive young woman with straight blond hair. The woman, wearing a pale yellow dress, looked vaguely familiar to Jessie.

"Your paintings are wonderful," Violet said shyly, as Grandfather introduced the children to Margaret Longford.

"Thank you." Margaret reached out to shake hands with Violet. "I hear painting is a hobby of yours."

"And she's good at it, too!" put in Benny. He sounded proud.

A flush of crimson crept over Violet's face. "I still have a lot to learn," she said modestly. "But I do love to draw and paint."

"That's what really matters," said Edmund. "When you look at Margaret's paintings, you just know she loves to paint more than anything in the world. You can see it in the brushstrokes and the vibrant colors. That's what makes her paintings so special."

"Just like Milly Manchester!" Benny chimed in. "Milly liked painting more than anything, too."

Margaret's smile suddenly faded. "I'm afraid I'm not familiar with that name." She seemed annoyed by Benny's remark. "I've never met Milly Manchester."

Edmund thought for a moment. "I believe she was a local painter." He looked over to where a middle-aged man was talking to a small group of people. "Isn't that her nephew, Jem Manchester?"

They followed Edmund's gaze to a man dressed in a checkered sports jacket and charcoal trousers. His dark hair was slicked back, and he was gesturing to the paintings with a sweep of his arm.

Just then, a voice said, "Yes, that's Jem." As Mrs. Turner joined their group, she told them, "He runs a car dealership in town."

Jessie caught Henry's eye. What was Jem Manchester doing at a gallery? According to Mrs. Spencer, Milly's nephew had no interest in art.

"I'm not surprised he's in sales," remarked Edmund. "He's quite the smooth talker. I overheard him praising Margaret's paintings, saying they'll be worth a fortune in a few years. Comments like that can't hurt business."

Margaret didn't look at all pleased. "My paintings will sell without anyone's help," she snapped. Then she turned on her heel and walked away.

Henry, Jessie, Violet, and Benny exchanged looks of amazement. Why was Margaret Longford so upset?

"I certainly didn't mean to insult anyone," Edmund remarked, puzzled.

"Margaret's from a wealthy family," put in Mrs. Turner. "She probably doesn't understand what it takes to run a business."

Edmund changed the subject. "I'll duck into the back room, James, and wrap that painting of yours." Then he hurried away.

Seeing the questioning look on the children's faces, Grandfather smiled over at them. "I bought one of the unframed canvasses," he told them. "I just couldn't resist. Margaret really is a brilliant artist."

"Mrs. Turner!" Jem Manchester suddenly came toward them, holding his hand out. "I had no idea you were a patron of the arts."

"I could say the same thing about you, Jem," she responded, shaking hands. Then she introduced the Aldens to Milly's nephew.

"The truth is, I've never spent much time in art galleries," Jem confessed, after saying hello to everyone. "But I wanted to find out what all the fuss was about. The whole town's doing cartwheels over Margaret Longford." He paused to glance around the room at the colorful canvasses. Slapping a hand over his heart, he said, "Her paintings have absolutely taken my breath away! Superb! No other word for it." Jem strode off, leaving everyone to stare after him.

Mrs. Turner laughed a little. "That's

quite a sales pitch he's giving. You'd almost think there was something in it for him, wouldn't you?"

When Edmund returned with Grandfather's painting, the Aldens thanked the gallery owner and said good-bye. As they were leaving, Jessie turned around for one last look at Margaret Longford. She still had the oddest feeling she'd seen her somewhere before. But she couldn't quite put her finger on where it was.

CHAPTER 8

A Snapdragon Lurks

When they got back from the gallery, Grandfather wasted no time in tearing the wrapping away from the painting he'd bought. He held up a landscape of clover fields edged with autumn trees that seemed to glow with light and color. In a bottom corner was Margaret Longford's signature.

Violet let out the breath she had been holding. "Oh, it's beautiful!" she said in an awed voice. And the others were quick to agree.

"I was hoping you'd like it, Violet." Grandfather smiled over at his youngest granddaughter. "I thought your bedroom would be the perfect place for it."

Violet gasped. "You bought this for . . . for me?" She looked as if she didn't quite believe it.

Nodding, Grandfather said, "I can't think of anyone who appreciates art more than you do."

"How can I ever thank you, Grandfather?" Violet gave him a warm hug.

James Alden chuckled. "The look on your face is all the thanks I need." Then he added, "I'll get Edmund to frame it for you after the exhibit."

"Your bedroom really is the perfect place for it, Violet," Jessie said, smiling happily at her sister.

"It sure is!" Henry was smiling, too.

"And don't forget," put in Benny, "it'll be worth a fortune in a few years. That's what Jem Manchester says."

Later, as the children sat in Violet's room,

Henry brought up something he had been thinking about.

"There's somebody else we might want to include on our list of Tattletale suspects," he said.

"Who is it?" they all asked at the same time.

"Mrs. Spencer."

"What . . . ?" The others were so surprised, all they could do was stare at their older brother.

"You don't really mean that, do you, Henry?" asked Jessie, who was sitting on the edge of Violet's bed. "You can't suspect Mrs. Spencer."

"We have to consider everybody."

"But why would she want to play a trick on us, Henry?" Violet couldn't believe Mrs. Spencer would do something so awful. "She's always been so nice to us."

"We all like her," said Henry, "but still . . . she could've planted all those clues herself. She wants her daughter to move in with her, remember? Maybe Rachel *will* move in if she thinks her mother's frightened by all the strange things that are happening."

They had to admit that it was possible. Didn't Mrs. Spencer want her daughter to go back to school and become a nurse? Wasn't moving in with her mother the only way Rachel could afford to do that?

"I still think our best suspect is Janice Allen," Violet insisted. "She even works at the gallery."

"*And* at the library," added Benny. "Don't forget, Mrs. Spencer likes to read. So Janice probably knows her." He thought for a minute. "I bet Janice knows everybody in Greenfield. She even knows Margaret Longford from school. Only . . . she calls her Peg."

Jessie clapped her hands. "Benny, you're brilliant!"

The youngest Alden was perched on the window seat, his arms wrapped around his knees. "Thank you," he said, grinning.

The others looked at Jessie, puzzled.

"I couldn't figure out where I'd seen her before," Jessie explained. "Margaret, I mean. Just now, when Benny mentioned the name Peg, it suddenly hit me. Margaret's the woman with the blond ponytail! She was in that snapshot with Milly."

"Mrs. Spencer *did* say her name was Peg," Henry realized. "I guess it could be the same person."

Benny looked doubtful. "Margaret said she'd never met Milly."

"We only got a quick look at that snapshot," said Violet, who was sitting right next to Jessie. "You can't be sure it was Margaret." Violet admired the young artist's work and didn't like to think she was dishonest.

"True," admitted Jessie. "There's no way of knowing for sure until we see the photograph again."

Henry got up from his chair. "If it *was* Margaret in the photo," he said in the middle of a yawn, "what do you think it means?"

"I don't know," replied Jessie, yawning, too. "I wish I did. Right now I'm too tired to think about it anymore."

It had been a long day, and the Aldens decided to get a good night's sleep.

Just before climbing into bed, Violet took one more admiring glance at Margaret's painting. But as she looked a little closer, she couldn't help noticing that the background was a different color around the edges of the canvas—almost as though the landscape had been painted over a finished work. It seemed odd to Violet. If Margaret was from a wealthy family, wouldn't she have enough money to buy new canvas? Why would she paint over another one of her paintings?

Violet was still wondering about it when she climbed into bed. But soon enough, she put it out of her mind as she closed her eyes and drifted off to sleep.

Leaving Watch with Mrs. McGregor, the Aldens rode their bikes over to Mrs. Spencer's the next morning. It wasn't long before their good friend was flipping through the pages of her photograph album.

"It's . . . it's gone!" cried Benny, as they all stared down at the empty space where the snapshot used to be. "The photograph has disappeared."

To their surprise, Mrs. Spencer did not seem at all shocked. "I'm sure it's around the house somewhere," she said matter-of-factly. "I must've taken it out for some reason." Brushing back wisps of her snowy white hair, she frowned a little. "I do hope I didn't misplace it. With everything that's been happening, I haven't been thinking clearly these days."

When the Aldens walked outside again, Violet said, "Poor Mrs. Spencer! I hope she finds her photograph."

"She won't find it, because Rachel stole it."

"Benny!" Jessie exclaimed. "You shouldn't say things like that!"

"But it's true," insisted Benny. "That day we met Rachel, I caught her looking through her mother's album. And I could tell by the look on her face that she was up to no good."

This made Henry smile a little. "Why would Rachel steal her mother's photo, Benny?"

"I don't know. But I'm pretty sure she did."

"I know Rachel wasn't very nice to us, Benny," said Violet, "but that doesn't make her a thief."

After a moment's thought, Jessie said, "It does seem odd, though, that the photograph suddenly disappeared."

Henry grinned over at his sister. "Remember what you said, Jessie? One mystery at a time."

At that, they voted to take another look around the gallery for clues. Hopping on their bikes, they headed for Town Square. When they arrived, they were surprised to find the gallery doing a brisk business even early in the day.

"Hi, kids!" Edmund called out as Henry, Jessie, Violet, and Benny came into the gallery. "What brings you here again to-day?"

"We were hoping to take another look at Margaret's paintings," Henry told the gallery owner. "If that's okay."

"Take all the time you want." As Edmund hurried away to greet a customer, he called back, "Hope you find what you're looking for."

Jessie and Henry exchanged glances. Did Edmund know they were looking for clues? Or was it just a coincidence he'd said that?

The Aldens kept their eyes peeled for anything unusual as they walked around the gallery . . . once . . . twice . . . three times. Sharp-eyed Benny was the first to notice something, and he was soon dashing from painting to painting.

Benny looked around to make sure no one would overhear him. Then he whispered to his brother and sisters what he'd discovered. "Margaret Longford put a snapdragon in all of her paintings, just like Milly!"

Henry looked puzzled. So did Jessie and Violet.

"What do you mean, Benny?" asked Henry.

It wasn't long before they were staring wide-eyed as their little brother led them from painting to painting. Sure enough, there was a bright pink snapdragon in every one!

Benny swallowed a bite of his toasted tomato sandwich. "So Margaret knew Milly after all."

The Aldens were sitting on cushions on the floor of the boxcar. They were talking about the mystery while they ate their lunch, with Watch curled up on his rug nearby.

"No doubt about it," said Henry. He wiped some mayonnaise from the corner of his mouth with a napkin. "It's not just a co-incidence Margaret put snapdragons in her paintings."

"That means she copied Milly," Benny said indignantly.

Henry nodded. "That's exactly what it means."

But Jessie wasn't so sure that's what it meant. Her mind was racing. "Unless . . ." A sudden thought came to her.

"Unless what, Jessie?" Violet questioned.

"Unless Milly's paintings weren't really destroyed in a fire."

The others looked at Jessie in surprise. "What do you mean?" Benny asked.

Jessie answered, "What if Jem just wanted everyone to think they were destroyed?"

This got Henry thinking. "Now that you mention it, Milly never signed her paintings. Margaret could've added her own signature to them easily."

"And then Milly's paintings could be sold," finished Jessie.

"Do you really think the paintings are Milly's?" Violet's eyes were huge.

Jessie nodded. "That would explain why Margaret lied about knowing her."

"I suppose so," Violet admitted reluctantly. She didn't want to believe Margaret would take credit for someone else's work.

But deep inside, she knew Jessie could be right.

Henry said, "It would also explain Jem's sudden interest in art." He crunched into an apple.

"And it proves someone stole the photograph," Benny added. "I bet Rachel is working with Jem and Margaret. They'll probably split the money they make from the paintings."

Henry couldn't argue. "You might be right, Benny. That photograph was the only evidence linking Margaret with Milly Manchester." He paused for a moment. "And Mrs. Spencer did say things are slow for Rachel at work. Maybe she saw Milly's paintings as a way to make some quick money."

"Mrs. Spencer will be so upset if her daughter really is involved in this," Jessie said, sighing.

"They would've gotten away with it, too, if it wasn't for a tattletale." Benny reached for one of Mrs. McGregor's homemade potato chips. "A tattletale by the name of Janice Allen, that is."

Henry had to admit it ruled out any possibility that Mrs. Spencer had planted the clues. It still seemed likely that Janice was the Tattletale. But if she knew Margaret had done something underhanded to win the contest, why wouldn't she just tell Edmund about it? After all, Janice had entered the contest, too, hadn't she? Something didn't add up.

"The problem is," Jessie put in, "how can we prove Milly's the real artist of the snapdragon paintings?"

Violet, who had been thinking quietly, spoke up. "I have an idea how we can prove it, but . . . it will depend on Grandfather."

The others stared at her, puzzled.

"What's your idea, Violet?" Benny asked, unable to keep the excitement out of his voice.

"I'd rather not say anything yet," Violet answered. "Just in case I'm on the wrong track."

The children quickly finished lunch, then

raced into the house to find Grandfather. As James Alden listened to his grandchildren, he looked more and more shocked.

"Even *this* painting might be one of Milly's," Violet was saying. She held up the landscape her grandfather had given her and pointed to a bright pink flower in the corner. "A snapdragon was Milly's only signature."

Grandfather got up from his desk and began to pace all around the den. "I can't believe this," he said. "If it's true, Margaret Longford has done a terrible thing."

Henry agreed. "She put her name on someone else's work."

Benny had something to add. "What about Jem Manchester? He's up to no good, too. His aunt didn't want him to sell her paintings."

Grandfather stopped pacing. "Are you sure you want to remove the top layer of paint, Violet?" He gave the landscape another admiring glance.

Violet nodded firmly. "I'm certain there's another painting underneath, Grandfather.

See how the background's a different color around the edges?" She ran her finger along the sides of the canvas. "If my hunch is right, there's something underneath that'll prove the paintings are Milly's."

Jessie added, "If we don't get proof soon, Milly's paintings will be gone."

"I've learned that my grandchildren's hunches are usually right. But it'll take an expert to remove that top layer of paint without damaging whatever's underneath." Grandfather gave the matter some thought. "I think Edmund Rondale is the man for the job."

Henry wasn't too sure about this. "But he's so busy with the art show this week. Do you think he'll have time to work on it?"

"Unless I miss my guess, Edmund will *make* time for it. After all, his gallery sponsored the art contest. And Edmund's an honest man. He'd want to put a stop to an artist passing off someone else's work as her own." With a sudden thought, Grandfather added, "I have an appointment downtown.

Why don't I drop the painting off at the gallery on my way."

"What do you think is under that landscape, Violet?" Benny asked after Grandfather had hurried away, the painting tucked under his arm.

"The real artist, Benny," Violet said, smiling mysteriously. "The real artist of the snapdragon paintings."

CHAPTER 9

Uncovering the Truth

It was almost dinnertime when Grandfather phoned, asking the children to meet him at the gallery right away. He sounded very mysterious.

The four Aldens got on their bicycles and pedaled as fast as they could to Town Square. When they arrived, they spotted Mrs. Spencer coming out of the bookstore.

Benny ran forward. "You'll never guess what, Mrs. Spencer," he cried, bursting with news. "We're on our way to the Mona Lisa Gallery—to solve the mystery!"

Mrs. Spencer gasped. "Really?"

"We can't be certain we'll solve it," Henry added honestly. "But we're keeping our fingers crossed."

"I can hardly believe this!" Mrs. Spencer's face broke into a big smile.

Jessie had a thought. "Why don't you come with us, Mrs. Spencer."

"Oh, yes!" urged Violet. "It would be so nice if you were there. Just in case we really do solve the mystery, I mean."

Mrs. Spencer was quick to agree. "I'm meeting Rachel for dinner. Just let me run and tell her what's happening," she said, pointing to the Greenfield Real Estate office. "Then I'll be right there." With a cheerful wave, she hurried off.

As soon as they were out of earshot, Violet said, "I hope Mrs. Spencer won't be disappointed."

Outside the gallery, Benny's shoulders suddenly slumped. "Uh-oh," he said. He took a step back and pointed to a sign in the window: CLOSED FOR DINNER. WILL OPEN AGAIN AT 7:00. "Looks like we're too late."

"Don't worry, Benny," Jessie assured him. "Grandfather said he'd be here."

No sooner had Jessie spoken than the door of the gallery swung open. "Hi, kids!" Janice Allen greeted them with a smile. "Your grandfather asked me to keep an eye out for you. He's in the back with Edmund," she said, ushering them inside.

Sure enough, the children found their grandfather in the back room, having a cup of coffee with the gallery owner.

"I knew you wouldn't waste any time," Grandfather said, smiling as they came into the room. "We were hoping you'd get here before the others." He looked relieved. So did Edmund.

"Others?" Henry looked surprised.

"Your grandfather suggested getting Margaret Longford and Jem Manchester over here on the double," explained Edmund. He was sipping his coffee, his shirtsleeves rolled up above his elbows. "I don't know what this is all about," he added, "but if something dishonest is going on around here, I want to get to the bottom of it."

The gallery owner gestured toward a large worktable covered with rags and bottles of solution. "I removed the top layer of paint from the landscape. Would you like to take a look at what I uncovered?"

When the Aldens nodded eagerly, Edmund went over to the worktable. He held up a portrait of an elderly woman with soft gray eyes and silver hair.

"Oh, wow!" Benny cried excitedly. "Milly Manchester!"

"Isn't that the self-portrait Milly was painting in Mrs. Spencer's snapshot?" Henry wondered, finding it hard to believe.

Jessie nodded. "I'm sure of it!" she said, astonished.

"That's the real artist of the snapdragon paintings." Violet didn't seem a bit surprised by what Edmund had uncovered.

"Self-portrait?" Edmund looked puzzled. "Milly Manchester painted this?" When the children nodded, he added, "But . . . why would Margaret paint over someone else's work?"

Henry spoke up. "We don't think it was Margaret who painted over it."

"Mrs. Spencer told us that Milly sometimes painted over her own finished work," explained Jessie. "If she was short of cash to buy new canvas, I mean."

Edmund put the portrait down. As he turned around, he raised a hand. "Wait a minute," he said. "Margaret Longford's signature was on the landscape." He looked at each of the Aldens in turn. "Surely you're not hinting that . . . that Margaret signed her name to someone else's work."

"We don't want to believe it," said Violet. "But it looks that way."

"And not just the landscape," put in Benny. "All the paintings in the gallery are Milly Manchester's."

"At least, that's what we think," added Jessie.

Edmund looked stunned. "I . . . I can't believe Margaret would do such a thing." He shook his head. "You must be mistaken."

"My grandchildren are seldom wrong

when it comes to solving mysteries," Grandfather said firmly.

As muffled sounds of conversation came from the gallery, Edmund rolled down his shirtsleeves. "I guess it's time to ask a few questions," he said, sighing deeply. Then, with a worried look on his face, he led the way out to the gallery, the portrait under his arm.

"What's this all about, Edmund?" Jem Manchester, who was standing with Margaret and Janice, was quick to confront the gallery owner. "You expect me to drop everything and come running down here on a moment's notice? I've got a business to run, too, you know!" He seemed a little rushed and out of breath.

"The next showing isn't until seven o'clock." Margaret sounded every bit as annoyed as Jem Manchester. "What's going on, Edmund?"

Benny put his hands on his hips. "Those paintings aren't supposed to be sold!" he blurted out.

Jem Manchester laughed, throwing back his head. "Now, that's a good one!"

"It's true," Benny said stubbornly. "Those are Milly Manchester's paintings."

A startled look crossed Margaret's face. But only for an instant. With an angry toss of her head, she turned to Edmund. "I certainly hope you didn't ask me down here to listen to this nonsense."

Jessie said, "Those *are* Milly's paintings. And we can prove it."

"Did you say . . . those are Milly's paintings?"

A voice behind them made everyone turn in surprise. It was Mrs. Spencer. She had just come into the gallery with her daughter. Jessie noticed Jem's eyes shift nervously when he caught sight of the elderly woman.

"It's true," said Henry, answering Mrs. Spencer's question. "Milly's the real artist."

Jem smiled over at the Alden children. "It's nice to see young people taking an interest in art," he said, although he didn't sound as if he meant it. "But you kids ought to get your facts straight before you go spouting off."

Henry squared his shoulders. "The fact is, Grandfather bought a landscape last night," he said, looking Jem straight in the eye. "Violet was sure there was another painting hidden under it, and — "

"There was!" finished Benny.

Nodding, Violet said in a quiet voice, "Edmund removed the top layer of paint, and he uncovered something that belongs to you, Mrs. Spencer."

As the gallery owner held up the portrait, Mrs. Spencer cried out in surprise.

Stepping forward, Rachel said, "Milly Manchester left that self-portrait to my mother in her will."

"If that's true, why was a landscape painted over it, Margaret?" Edmund demanded. "A landscape with your signature on it."

Margaret didn't answer right away. She took a deep breath and tried to collect her thoughts. Finally she blurted out, "It's not a self-portrait at all. I was the one who painted that picture of Milly. But I never *did* care much for it." She shrugged a little. "That's why I painted over it. What's wrong with that?" she added rather sharply.

"Why would you paint a picture of somebody you didn't know?" Benny asked, accusingly.

It was a good question. Margaret had made it clear she'd never met Milly Manchester. Why would she paint her portrait? Everyone waited expectantly for an answer.

Margaret struggled to find something to say. "I . . . I meant I didn't know Milly very well. She gave me a few tips on painting, that's all."

The Aldens looked at one another in surprise. They had been certain Margaret would confess when she saw Milly's self-portrait. They hadn't counted on her trying to bluff her way out of it.

But Henry wasn't giving up so easily. "What about the snapdragons?"

Margaret blinked. "What . . . ?"

"There's a snapdragon in every one of those paintings," stated Henry, watching Margaret closely.

Mrs. Spencer glanced around at the gallery walls. "Then they really *are* Milly's paintings," she said in an awed voice. "That was Milly's signature, you know — a bright pink snapdragon."

Edmund looked grim. "There seem to be some strange things going on around here."

"I'll tell you what's strange." Jem seemed amused. "It's strange anybody would think those are my aunt's paintings." Then he shook his head sadly. "Her canvasses were destroyed in a fire, you know. Every last one of them. Such a terrible loss!"

"Maybe that's just what you want everyone to believe," Henry suggested.

Jem pretended to look hurt. "How can you accuse me of such a thing? I'm a respectable businessman. Why, that would be . . ."

"Dishonest?" finished Grandfather.

"Unless you can *prove* what you're saying," Jem responded in an icy voice, "we have nothing more to discuss."

Edmund glanced over at Jem a little suspiciously, but did not say anything. Then Jessie caught a knowing look pass between Janice and Rachel.

Janice suddenly spoke up. "I believe I can prove it," she said. "I have something in my purse I think you should see, Edmund." With that, Janice disappeared into the back room. She returned a moment later, waving a photograph in the air.

Edmund's face grew grim as he studied the snapshot. After a lengthy silence, he looked up. "How would you explain this, Margaret?" he demanded, passing the photograph to her. "As you can see, it clearly shows Milly Manchester painting her own portrait—with you watching nearby."

Margaret's face turned very red as she looked down at the snapshot.

"That sounds like your photograph, Mrs. Spencer," observed Benny. "The one that was missing from your album."

"But how in the world did — " Mrs. Spencer began.

Rachel interrupted. "I'll explain everything to you later," she whispered. And she gave her mother a reassuring pat on the back.

Jem inched his way closer to Margaret and looked over her shoulder. As he got a glimpse of the photograph, his mouth dropped open.

"Well, Margaret," Edmund said sternly. "What do you have to say for yourself?"

Margaret didn't answer. Instead, she wheeled around to face Jem. "This is all your fault!" she cried, almost shouting. "I told you not to come to the gallery. Didn't I warn you it would look too suspicious? But oh, no, you had to come anyway, didn't you? You just couldn't resist giving one of your big sales pitches." Margaret shook her finger at him. "You're a fool, Jem Manchester! Your aunt was a brilliant artist. Her paintings would've sold without any help from you."

Jem's eyes darted from side to side. He

opened his mouth several times as if about to speak, then closed it again. Finally he let out a sigh and said, "All right, it's true. My aunt painted every last one of them. But she had no business putting a condition in her will!" He sounded upset. "There's nothing wrong with a guy wanting to make a few bucks. I should've been able to do whatever I wanted with her paintings!"

He stopped talking for a moment. Then he gave a little shrug. "Anyway, no harm done," he said, suddenly trying to make light of everything. "Why don't I just gather up my paintings and get out of your way." Then, with a few quick strides, he went over and took a painting down from the wall.

But Mrs. Spencer wasn't having any of that. "Not so fast, Jem Manchester! Aren't you forgetting something? As I recall, Milly's will makes it clear that if you try to sell her art, her paintings become the property of the Greenfield Public Library."

Replacing the painting, Jem headed for the door, muttering to himself. As he left, he called out, "You won't be seeing me in here again!"

"I'll count on it," replied Edmund.

When the door slammed shut, the gallery owner turned to Margaret. "I can't believe you'd take credit for someone else's work," he said. "How could you do something like that?" Edmund sounded more disappointed than angry.

Rachel had an opinion about this. "For the money, no doubt." She shook her head in disappoval. "Just like Jem Manchester."

Margaret's dark eyes suddenly flashed. "That's not true! Every dime from those paintings was going to Jem," she shot back. "It was always about the money with him. It never was for me."

Edmund lifted his hands in bewilderment. "Then . . . why?"

Violet thought she knew the answer. "You wanted to make a name for yourself in the art world, didn't you?"

Margaret looked down shamefully. "Yes, I did want to make a name for myself," she acknowledged. "My family always told me I was wasting my time painting. They wanted me to follow in my father's footsteps and become a lawyer." She swallowed hard. "I figured if I could win the art contest and get some good reviews from the art critics, my career would take off, and my family would finally accept my decision to become an artist."

"So you went along with Jem's plan to sell his aunt's paintings," concluded Jessie.

Margaret didn't deny it. "I was shocked when Jem first mentioned it. Milly had taught me so much, and she'd always been so kind to me." Her voice wavered. "I just couldn't imagine betraying her like that — passing her work off as my own. I told Jem I wouldn't do it. And I meant it, too."

"But then you changed your mind," put in Henry, urging her on.

"I really didn't want to do it." Margaret looked close to tears. "But my father refused to pay for my art studies at the college anymore. I was desperate to prove to him I could make it as an artist."

Margaret told the rest of the story

quickly. Jem had concocted a scheme to make everyone believe his aunt's works of art had been destroyed in a fire. Then Margaret signed her name to the paintings and entered them in the art contest sponsored by the Mona Lisa Gallery. It seemed simple enough. After all, Milly had never put her paintings on display anywhere, so very few people had ever seen them.

"Jem's plan seemed foolproof," finished Margaret. "So I agreed."

"Nothing's ever foolproof, Margaret," said Edmund. "Now you'll have to suffer the consequences of your actions." His voice was stern. "It'll be a long time before the art world will trust you again."

Margaret didn't have a reply to that. She just hung her head and stared at the floor.

Janice spoke up. "If you really want to stay in the art program, Margaret, you could put yourself through school. Lots of people do. Of course, it's not easy working *and* going to school," she added. "But it's worth it."

"I . . . I never thought of doing it on my

own," Margaret said, a faint note of hope in her voice.

Mrs. Spencer had something to add. "Milly thought you were a fine painter, Margaret. She always hoped you'd develop your own style one day."

"Milly was always a good friend to me," said Margaret. She stood twisting her hands. "I'm so ashamed of what I've done." Looking truly regretful, she turned and walked slowly from the gallery.

CHAPTER 10

Gotcha!

"I can't believe it!" said Mrs. Spencer, shaking her head in wonder. "Thanks to the Aldens, I can finally hang Milly's portrait on my wall."

After leaving the gallery, Edmund had invited everyone to join him at Cooke's Drugstore for a quick bite to eat. Now Mrs. Spencer, Rachel, Janice, Edmund, Grandfather, and the children were sitting together at the long counter, feasting on huge bowls of Mrs. Turner's chili.

"Uncovering that portrait was a surprise

to everyone," Jessie admitted. Then she gave her sister an affectionate nudge. "Everyone except Violet, that is."

"It was just a hunch," Violet said modestly as Mrs. Turner filled her water glass. "I was fairly sure there was another painting under that landscape. And I remembered that Milly might have painted over her self-portrait. At least that's what Mrs. Spencer thought."

"That was great thinking," Henry praised his sister.

Swallowing a bite of his roll, Benny said, "But now you don't have a painting for your room, Violet."

"The important thing," said Violet, smiling over at her little brother, "is that now Mrs. Spencer has Milly's portrait to hang on her wall."

"What wonderful grandchildren you have, James!" Mrs. Spencer remarked.

Grandfather smiled proudly. "You won't get any argument from me!"

"I'll have that portrait framed for you right away, Mrs. Spencer," Edmund promised. He reached out and patted the elderly woman's hand. "It's the least I can do after all that's happened. And, of course, you'll get your money back for that landscape, James." Edmund sighed. "I can't help but feel partly responsible for what Jem and Margaret tried to do. After all, it was *my* gallery that sponsored the contest."

"Nobody blames you, Edmund," Grandfather assured him. "Everyone in town knows you're an honest man."

Edmund held out his cup as Mrs. Turner poured the coffee. "Jem's plan *was* almost foolproof," he remarked. "Of course, he didn't count on the Aldens coming along and figuring everything out."

"They're first-class detectives, that's for sure!" said Grandfather.

"We like solving mysteries," said Benny. The other Aldens agreed.

But they knew the mystery was still not fully explained. They still weren't sure who the Tattletale was.

Henry spoke up. "There's something I don't understand. You entered the art contest, right, Janice?" When she nodded in reply, he questioned, "Then why did you tell us you couldn't draw?"

"I did say that, didn't I?" Janice smiled a little. "I guess I was feeling a bit discouraged at the time. You see, I had my hopes pinned on winning that contest. When it didn't happen, I began to wonder if I was just kidding myself about making it as an artist."

"Your paintings show real talent, Janice," Edmund assured her. "There's no reason to doubt yourself."

Benny had a question for Janice, too. "How did you know Watch's name?"

Janice looked puzzled.

"In the Town Square," Benny explained, "you called Watch by his name. But you'd never met him before."

Janice laughed. "You're the clue to that one, Benny. You got a book from the library about dogs a while ago. Remember? When you were checking it out, you told me all about Watch."

Benny grinned sheepishly. "I forgot about that."

Henry and Jessie looked at each other. If Janice wasn't the Tattletale, who was? Could Benny have been right all along? Was the ghost of Milly Manchester behind everything?

"Something baffles me, too," put in Mrs. Spencer. "How did you ever get hold of that snapshot of mine, Janice?"

Benny thought he knew the answer. "Rachel probably gave it to her."

"Right," said Rachel, looking surprised that Benny knew that. "Milly's portrait meant so much to you, Mother, I decided to do something about it. When I heard Janice was in the art program at the college, I asked her if she'd paint another portrait for you."

"But I had no idea what Milly looked like," put in Janice. "I'd never even met her."

Rachel nodded. "She needed a snapshot. So I took one from your album when you weren't looking, Mother. I wanted the portrait to be a surprise."

"But now you have the original portrait,

Mrs. Spencer," Janice pointed out. "Nothing can be better than that."

"I'm sorry for being so unfriendly the other day," Rachel said, smiling over at the children. She was a changed person now that the mystery was solved. "I was upset about the strange things that were happening to my mother. I'm afraid I thought it was just a game to you."

"It was never just a game to us," said Jessie, shaking her head firmly. "We wanted to help."

Still smiling, Rachel said, "I know that now. Because of you, my mother can hang Milly's portrait on her wall."

"And don't forget," added Janice, "the library has a beautiful new art collection. Now everyone in Greenfield can enjoy Milly's paintings."

Grandfather nodded. "Jem's loss is the town's gain."

"That man sees nothing but dollar signs!" Mrs. Turner suddenly blurted out as she refilled the saltshaker. "I'm not surprised he planned to keep all the money for himself.

Can you imagine? Not a penny to go into Margaret's pockets."

When he heard this, Henry was suddenly alert. "How did you know that, Mrs. Turner?" he asked suspiciously. The other Alden children were wondering the same thing.

The question seemed to catch the waitress off guard. "What . . . ?"

Henry said, "How did you know they weren't planning to split the money?"

The saltshaker suddenly slipped from Mrs. Turner's hand, spilling salt onto the counter.

"Oh, dear, now what have I done?" The waitress looked flustered. "I'll just go get a cloth. I'll have this wiped up in a jiffy." She turned and quickly walked away.

"That was a bit strange, don't you think?" Henry looked at Jessie, then over at Violet and Benny.

Jessie nodded. "I'll say."

"Something just doesn't seem right," Henry told them, keeping his voice low. He took another spoonful of chili and chewed thoughtfully. It was almost as if Mrs. Turner knew, somehow, about Jem and Margaret's plans. Was she hiding something?

Henry suddenly had a thought that hadn't occurred to him before. Reaching into his pocket, he pulled out the gold hair clip, the one he had found in Mrs. Spencer's garden. On a hunch that it just might come in handy, he had thought to bring it along.

"Is this yours, Mrs. Turner?" he asked, holding it up when Mrs. Turner returned.

The waitress smiled broadly. "I've been looking everywhere for that!" Taking the hair clip, she slipped it into her apron pocket. "Thank you, Henry. Where in the world did you find it?"

"In Mrs. Spencer's backyard," Henry answered, watching her closely.

A funny look came over Mrs. Turner's face. "Oh . . . that's quite impossible. Why, I've never been anywhere near — "

Henry cut in, "Maybe you lost it when you were planting that snapdragon in Mrs. Spencer's pansy bed."

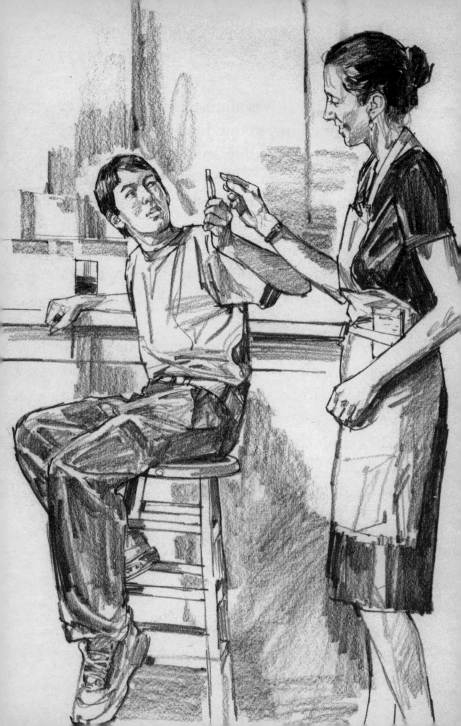

Without saying a word, Mrs. Turner busied herself wiping away the spilled salt. It was as if she hadn't even heard Henry's remark. A moment later, though, her cheeks turned bright pink as she became aware of everyone watching her.

"It all adds up," Henry went on. "You were at our house the day the paper airplane flew into our yard."

"And you were at the art show, too," Benny realized.

Jessie was thinking hard. "You even made a comment about Jem. You said he was acting as if there were something in it for him. You were trying to give us a hint, weren't you, Mrs. Turner?"

The waitress still said nothing.

"You gave us another hint, too," recalled Violet, "when you pointed to the pigeon on Josiah Wade's head. You were trying to draw our attention to the minuteman statue, weren't you?"

After a long silence, Mrs. Turner finally spoke. "I knew you kids were real pros, but I wasn't counting on this," she said with a sigh. "I had no idea you'd figure out I was the Tattletale."

"Oh!" Mrs. Spencer cried out in surprise, putting her hands to her mouth. And the others looked just as astonished.

Mrs. Turner began speaking quietly. "Milly used to stop by the drugstore for a cup of coffee. We'd always have such nice chats. She knew everything there was to know about the history of art. She especially loved talking about Leonardo da Vinci. It was fascinating just to listen to her." Mrs. Turner stopped to tighten the lid on the saltshaker. "Milly told me how a snapdragon in a pansy bed made her realize that anything's possible in life. She even drew a sketch of a snapdragon for me. I kept it just to remind me of what Milly had said — that anything's possible."

"But then you wrote a message on the back of the sketch," guessed Violet, "and you folded it into a paper airplane. Right?"

"Right." Mrs. Turner nodded. "I was planning to leave the message somewhere in the house that day. But you kids were flying paper airplanes in the backyard. On a whim, I sent the message to you like that." The waitress looked over at Mrs. Spencer. "I'm afraid it's true. I planted the snapdragon in your garden when you were out one day. I sent the coded message in the mail. And I tucked that bookmark inside your book one afternoon in the park." She sighed deeply. "The bookmark was one Milly made for me on my birthday."

"Then you wanted it to look like Milly was doing all these things?" Mrs. Spencer asked, disbelieving.

Nodding, Mrs. Turner lowered her eyes. "I didn't want anyone to suspect I was the Tattletale. And yet . . . I had to let somebody know about Jem and Margaret. So what else could I do?" She didn't look as if she expected an answer.

"How did you know what they were up to?" asked Rachel.

"They were in here planning the whole thing over lunch. I heard every word. But I really didn't think they'd go through with it. Later, I found out Margaret had won the art contest and I knew they'd carried out their plan."

After a moment's stunned silence, Edmund said, "Why didn't you just tell someone about it? Why all the elaborate clues?"

"When you're a waitress, you overhear things," Mrs. Turner confided. "You really can't help it, you know. I think my customers forget I have ears." She paused for a moment. "When I first started working here, I didn't know how to hold my tongue. I'm afraid I had a reputation for being a gossip."

The children looked surprised to hear this.

Mrs. Turner went on, "It wasn't long before my customers were calling me Turner the Tattletale. Oh, it took me years to live that down! After that, I promised myself that never again would I repeat something I overheard."

The Aldens nodded as they began to understand. Nobody liked being called names.

Benny looked puzzled. "But, Mrs. Turner, why did you use that name when you signed the messages? If you didn't like being called a tattletale, I mean."

"I was telling secrets about people again, Benny." A sad smile crossed Mrs. Turner's face. "The name just seemed to fit."

"But you couldn't just stand by and let Milly's paintings be sold," insisted Janice.

"Sometimes being a tattletale isn't such a bad thing," Violet added softly. "Not if you know somebody's doing something wrong."

Mrs. Turner nodded, but she looked troubled. "Still . . . I hope you won't mention my role in all of this," she said. "You see, I don't want to hear that name Turner the Tattletale again. Not ever!"

"You did everyone a great service, Mrs. Turner," Grandfather said, speaking for them all. "Your secret's safe with us."

Mrs. Turner looked relieved.

"And I'll return that bookmark," Mrs. Spencer told her. "After all, it was a gift from Milly."

Edmund took a napkin from the dispenser. "I wish I'd known Milly Manchester," he said. "She must've been a remarkable person to make such an impression on so many people."

Mrs. Spencer nodded. "She was one of a kind."

"Milly followed her dream, and she never let anything stand in her way," Rachel commented thoughtfully. Then suddenly she turned to her mother. Taking a deep breath, she said, "If that offer's still open, I just might take you up on it and move back home for a while."

"Oh, you'll make a wonderful nurse, Rachel!" Mrs. Spencer looked close to tears. She reached out and gave her daughter's hand a gentle squeeze. "It's never too late to follow your dreams."

For a moment, nobody said a word. Then Edmund spoke up. "I think this calls for a celebration. How about dessert all around?" he suggested. "Any takers?"

"It just so happens I make a great chocolate sundae," put in Mrs. Turner.

Benny grinned. "With extra sprinkles?"

"You'd better believe it!" answered Mrs. Turner.

"I bet that's why Mona Lisa was smiling," said Benny. "I bet she was thinking about a chocolate sundae with — "

"Extra sprinkles!" everyone finished in unison.

GERTRUDE CHANDLER WARNER discovered when she was teaching that many readers who like an exciting story could find no books that were both easy and fun to read. She decided to try to meet this need, and her first book, *The Boxcar Children*, quickly proved she had succeeded.

Miss Warner drew on her own experiences to write the mystery. As a child she spent hours watching trains go by on the tracks opposite her family home. She often dreamed about what it would be like to set up housekeeping in a caboose or freight car — the situation the Alden children find themselves in.

When Miss Warner received requests for more adventures involving Henry, Jessie, Violet, and Benny Alden, she began additional stories. In each, she chose a special setting and introduced unusual or eccentric characters who liked the unpredictable.

While the mystery element is central to each of Miss Warner's books, she never thought of them as strictly juvenile mysteries. She liked to stress the Aldens' independence and resourcefulness and their solid New England devotion to using up and making do. The Aldens go about most of their adventures with as little adult supervision as possible — something else that delights young readers.

Miss Warner lived in Putnam, Connecticut, until her death in 1979. During her lifetime, she received hundreds of letters from girls and boys telling her how much they liked her books.